# NO!

Tracey Corderoy

Tim Warnes

LITTLE TIGER PRESS
London

Archie was adorable.
Everybody said so . . .

Then Archie learned
a brand new word...

Archie loved his brand new word.
So he said it more and more.

He said it at mealtimes...

He said it at
bath times...

And he said it at
every single bedtime...

When it was time to go out Archie got himself ready.

But would he put his coat on?

Archie practised his new favourite word at nursery...

Shall I take your lunchbox, Archie?

No!

Unfortunately, that
didn't go so well...

Soon Archie was saying his word **all** the time. But sometimes he wished he hadn't...

Come and join our train, Archie!

No!

Hey, where's everybody gone?

As time went on, his little word became a big, **big** problem . . .

We'd better go in now. It's going to rain!

NO!

Feed me!

At home time, Daddy asked,
"Have you had a nice day?"
Archie gave a little sniff.

"Would you like a hug?" said Daddy.
"N-nnnnn . . ."

WAAAH!

Now Archie had a
**new** favourite word ...

Hey, Archie!
Would you like
to play?